SANGUINE

SIERRA SIMONE

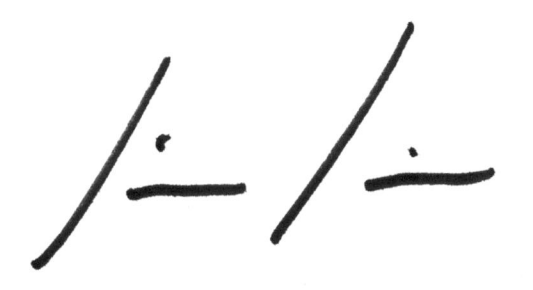

Copyright © 2023 by Sierra Simone

All rights reserved.

No part of this book may be reproduced in any form or by any electronic or mechanical means, including information storage and retrieval systems, without written permission from the author, except for the use of brief quotations in a book review.

Without in any way limiting the author's and publisher's exclusive rights under copyright, any use of this publication to "train" generative artificial intelligence (AI) technologies to generate text is expressly prohibited. The author reserves all rights to license uses of this work for generative AI training and development of machine learning language models.

WANT TO LISTEN TO SANGUINE FOR FREE?

Don't miss Shane East's toe-curling narration of *Sanguine*, complete with the most delicious accents! Scan the QR code below to download the free audiobook!

SANGUINE

CHAPTER 1

BASTIEN

I GENERALLY LIKE PRIESTS, even when they're trying to kill me.

But I'm really not in the fucking mood this morning.

I can feel the warm kiss of the sunlight through the open folding doors, and I can hear the gentle churn of the Coral Sea outside—it's time to *sleep*, not deal with holy men scratching at my gates, and anyway, the whole reason I rented this place on Hamilton Island was so I could have a few months of peace, which I think I've earned, and I've especially earned the right not to be vexed by a self-righteous butcher, and all I want to do is sleep curled up in this sunbeam like a cat, and is that so much to ask?

After the buzzer rings the third time, I reach for my phone and open the security app to answer it. "Fuck off. And if you're here to kill me, extra fuck off."

"I'm not here to kill you." The voice on the other end of the line is impatient, as if *I'm* the problem here, even though he's the one rudely waking me up to murder me.

"I don't believe you," I say crisply. "Now please go away."

"We both know," the voice says, "that I can be inside the house in the next five minutes anyway. Unlike you, I don't need an invitation to enter, so you may as well let me in."

I think about this for a moment. The house is surrounded with stone walls and gates, but they're more to limit the gaze of tourists (and their smartphones) and paparazzi (and their cameras) than to stop serious intruders. Or priests on a mission.

"I can call security," I say.

"You can," the voice agrees.

It's Australian, that voice, although not broadly so. Just some pleasantly relaxed vowels and a slight lilt to the end of his sentences.

Damn that friendly accent, I can't tell whether he's telling the truth or not.

"*Ugh*," I say—not into my phone, just into the warm, sea-scented air.

I came to the Whitsundays to relax! To splash around in the water! To drink some nice Australian wine! And yes, fine, to bite the suntanned necks of happy tourists, but that's really immaterial to the point. Don't I deserve a vacation? Don't I deserve an infinity pool with ocean views?

"Fine," I say irritably—to the priest this time, not just

my room. "You can come in. But maybe I'll kill *you*, have you ever thought of that?"

"I'm not here to kill you," the priest repeats, mostly without inflection, although I still hear the thread of impatience in his voice. Like he's already late for an appointment and taking the time to kill me is making him even later.

Ugh, fuck this guy. I have stuff I'd rather be doing too! Like sleeping!

I mutter a pissy noise into the phone—not strictly necessary, but I want him to know how annoyed I am—and I press the gate button. As it opens, I pull up the camera view to get an idea of his size. Not that I've ever had a problem fighting off priests—a tribe of paper-skinned elders and their scrawny, still-pimpled pupils—but it's good to know one's enemy and all that.

But I'm too late with the camera view. I just get a glimpse of silver-white hair as the priest moves past the gate and onto the narrow path crowded by exuberant tropical plants. An old man.

Please go away, I think as I push myself out of bed and tug on some linen pants. As grumbly and tired as I am, I still don't want to kill anyone. I've never liked killing, even when it was necessary, and I certainly don't like killing priests. Or old men.

Maybe I can scare him enough that he won't come back. Although if I know priests, I know that he will come back, and that's—sigh—a thing. A real thing that would be close to a problem, and I'm so very tired of problems.

Don't make me kill you, old man.

I pad to the door and open it before he can knock—and then freeze. Because I am not looking at an old man.

There're a few lines around his eyes, but that's not surprising for someone with fair skin as sun-kissed as his. The hair—the hair *is* near-white, but up close, I can see it's a very particular shade of blond, and it hangs to his shoulders in a sort of careless tousle that I like very much.

And his face ... it's the face of a man past true youth and into his prime—but not by very much. Stubble shadows a square jaw, a shallow cleft winks from his chin, and bright amber eyes stare at me from beneath heavy brows. He can't be much more than thirty-two or thirty-three, but those eyes look at me with the weary acceptance of someone three times his age.

Although as he takes me in—my face, my exposed chest and stomach, my bare feet—the expression in those haunting eyes changes somewhat. Heats into something less weary that could be lust or could be loathing, it's hard to say. I often inspire both in people.

The Australian priest is big, massive, a rock wall of a man—six and a half feet, shoulders filling the doorway—and I find myself appreciating the brutal, holy hulk of him as I take a step backward onto the balls of my feet. I'm very strong—I was before I changed, being not too much shorter than the Viking in front of me, and now I'm an apex predator anyway—but even I might have trouble with this one.

He sees my movement, and his amber eyes flash from

my feet back up to my face. "I told you I wasn't here to kill you."

"I've heard it before, priest," I say, a tad crankily. (But I really have heard it before. Usually before the stake and mallet come out.)

For the first time since I opened the door, he looks surprised. "I'm not a priest."

I don't even have enough scoffs to scoff properly at that. "Please. I could sense you all the way from the gate."

His lips part. They are wonderful lips, as firm and sculpted as the rest of him, with two well-defined peaks and the shallowest possible curve to the bottom lip. All grim geometry, this priest's face. It's very hard not to want to lick it.

"You could ... *sense* me?" he asks, sounding unnerved.

I decide he's probably not going to kill me immediately, and also that a holy man in my house at this bright hour calls for something to drink, so I turn on my heel and stride into the kitchen. "You know what I am, and yet you're asking me this question?"

He follows me to the kitchen—first closing the front door, which I find a rather touching commitment to manners, all things considered—and then stands across the glistening expanse of kitchen island from me as I start chopping fruit for a nice sangria. He looks around before answering me, and while his face stays unreadable, there's no disguising the quick, saccadic movements of his eyes as they log every detail of this paradisiacal nest.

The house is a lovely, open-plan type thing, with one central kitchen-cum-dining-room-cum-living-room, and it spills out onto a shaded terrace, which then extends out to the infinity pool. As I have since I first came here, I have all the windows and folding glass doors open, letting in the breeze and ceaseless spill of the ocean outside. Dent Island is rucked up around the horizon, like a dark green quilt kicked to the bottom of a bed, and cottony clouds waft above like overfluffed pillows. The pool is a rippling, Impressionist painting of it all, a painting set right into the lush, emerald-green lawn.

Everything inside the house is gleaming wood and generous furniture; it's tailor-made for a billionaire and their paramour, or maybe a celebrity and their entourage, but of course I'm knocking about in it alone, wasteful rake that I am. And the priest doesn't hide the moment this registers with him. "You're by yourself," he says.

"And you never answered my question." I finish chopping the lemons and oranges and move to the apples. "You know I'm a vampire, and yet you don't know we can sense priests? How have you survived this long?"

I'm genuinely curious. He's not surprised to see me moving through sunlight or popping the occasional apple chunk into my mouth, which means he knows more about vampires than most people. He knows we're mammals, not magic, and that our eyes are better suited to hunting at night, so while we skew nocturnal, the sunlight doesn't hurt us any more than it hurts a cat or an owl. He knows the combination of electrolytes, glucose, lipids and iron in human blood is the only complete meal for us—but we still eat and drink other things too.

"I'm not a priest," the man repeats. And then pauses. "Anymore."

"Aha!" I say through a bite of apple, pointing my knife at him. "J'accuse!"

Those eyes flash again. A thrill runs right down my spine, as if a lion had just locked stares with me. I'm not the only predator in this room, and I'd put my not inconsiderable money on him having been a vampire hunter in his time. Some self-destructive part of me idly wonders what it would be like to see those eyes flashing up at me as I pinned him to my bed ... or as he crawled over me, so big he blocked out all the light except whatever was reflected from his gaze...

"That chapter of my life is closed," the man says. "It was a long time ago."

"I bet it won't seem like a long time to me, and also, I don't care what Rome thinks, you're still a priest."

A growl rumbles in his chest as he takes a step forward. I think I feel that growl from the nape of my neck to the lazily stirring length in my drawstring pants.

"I'm. *Not*."

I set the knife down and find a glass pitcher. "Do you know how vampires suspect a priest is near?" I grab an opened bottle of red wine and pour it in. An obnoxious *glug glug glug* noise fills the kitchen. "We have superior senses in almost every way. Truly superhuman. I can smell fear, for example, and I can hear lust—and in your case, I can perceive in every single possible way your clarity, your faith, and your devotion. It brightens the air around you, and it makes the space near you hum. I can taste your faith, and it tastes like"—I close my eyes and savor him on my tongue for a moment—"ironically, it tastes like communion. The wafers, I mean. It's the serotonin in your body. The dopamine too. It's so close to being sweet, but the moment you apprehend the sweetness, it dissolves. Beckoning you back, urging you to take more. Begging to be chased. Much like God Himself, if I may say so."

I open my eyes and get back to the sangria, adding the orange juice.

The man stares at me, lips parted again.

"None of that has gone away," I tell him, adding the fruit to the wine and then hunting for some brandy. "Maybe you no longer wear a collar, but inside, you're still a man of God. I'm not sure why you left the Church —or why you were kicked out—but lack of faith wasn't the reason." I find a cinnamon stick, swirl it in the pitcher with some flair. "Ta-da! Do you want some? Of course you do, you're Catholic and there're only golf buggies on this island, so who cares about drinking—here's a glass now, stop being so shy."

The ex-priest sniffs at the glass, then raises those wonderful eyes to mine. "It's only wine? Nothing ... else?"

I roll my eyes. "This isn't Gilded Age Paris, mon ami; I'm not stocking my cellar with casks of human blood in between visits to the opera. It's just wine."

"Hmm."

"You have to admit a priest who's worried about blood in his wine is *deeply ironic*."

"Hmm."

"Also can I just point out the Latin root of 'sangria'? From 'sanguis,' meaning blood. So in a linguistic sense, we are drinking blood, am I right?"

I don't think I've ever seen anyone as serious as the man in front of me, even after being exposed to the full force of my linguistic wit.

But he does take a tentative sip, then licks his lips after, which sends my already interested cock into *very obviously* interested territory.

And then when he takes a real drink, and I watch the swallow work its way down his throat, I nearly have a heart attack. If I had my lips on that neck, if I had my teeth there …

I have to move around the corner of the island so he doesn't see the needy erection currently pressing against my pants. They're loose enough pants but they're also thin, and also—this isn't to brag, it's honestly just true—it's a very noticeable cock when it's in the mood.

The man sets the glass carefully on the counter, as if one drink of wine will be quite enough, thank you very much. "You're not how I thought you would be," he says after a minute.

I'm trying not to think about his throat. Or the way a drop of wine lingers on his lower lip, begging to be sucked off. "And how did you think I was going to be?"

He shrugs. "I've met some vampires before. They weren't as…blithe…as you are."

"Blithe?" I echo, a smile growing across my face. "*Blithe*? That's the word you picked?"

The man grunts, and if I'm not mistaken, there's color coming up on his cheeks. "It's a real word," he mutters defensively. "I've read it before."

"First of all, can we just acknowledge that not using 'sanguine' was a real missed opportunity for you, given our discussion five seconds ago about Latin root words?"

"I like blithe," he says. Stubbornly.

I'm shaking my head and laughing. This silver-haired giant looks like he could crush rocks with his bare hands —and then out he comes with *blithe*. "Got any other thesaurus words for me? Jocund, maybe? Mirthful? Merry? Gladsome? Gay?"

The word *gay* makes his cheeks go even pinker. Interesting.

"Let me ask you this, Mr. Ex-Priest: were you a hunter? Because if the only vampires you met were vampires you killed, then that probably explains why they weren't so blithe when they met you. When we're not fighting for our lives, we do tend to be a fairly sunny bunch. Get it? *Sunny?* You're not laughing. You're one of those austere Latin Mass priests, aren't you?"

"I was a hunter," he says, ignoring my last question. "But I left because I didn't want to hunt anymore."

"So you're not hunting me now?" I ask.

He shakes his head. The ends of his silvery-blond hair brush distractingly over his shoulders. They're *big* shoulders, big and hard, and I wish I could squeeze them. From behind.

While I pressed slow and slick into his muscular body.

"I didn't come to hurt you," he says, and when he looks at me this time, there's a sort of earnestness underneath the grim sphinx thing he has going on. Like he wants me to believe him. "I came because I saw you last night, and I—" He clears his throat, pauses, clears his throat again. He looks very uncomfortable, and I'm already guessing why.

"You saw me hunt," I say. Flatly. "And even though it's not your job to stop me anymore, you feel like you need to—what? Chastise me for it? Threaten me away? Chase me off?"

"No," he says, more quickly than he's spoken all day. "Nothing like that. You didn't kill him—and you took so much less than you needed."

"I never kill, not if I can help it," I inform him, my blithe mood gone. (I'm a little sensitive about this, if you can't tell). "I haven't killed since—well, okay, it was Gilded Age Paris actually—but that was *provoked* and everyone I've told the story to agrees with me, if you must know. I just want to drink and then let my victims go, no worse off than if they'd donated blood. Which, I mean, really is what it amounts to if you think about it."

The pink is back in his cheeks. I blink at him, wondering why seeing me hunt last night would be embarrassing for him—*oh*. Ohhhhhhhh.

Oh yeah. This priest is getting very interesting indeed.

I give him my wickedest, most louche grin. "You saw more than the drinking, didn't you? You saw the *kissing*."

"Do you—" He clears his throat again. "Do you

always kiss them? Your victims?"

"When they want me to." I fold my arms across my chest, suddenly back to enjoying this morning very much. All this delicate blushing on such a big, bleak man—it's a combination of delights, enticing and carnal. I wonder if I could bite that blush sometime, just a little nip, just a sharp, little kiss. "Why do you ask, my sullen priest? Are you in the market to be kissed? Or bitten?"

He shifts, and although his body ripples with unconscious grace, I can also sense his uneasiness. A light lace of adrenaline and cortisol in his blood, making the air around him taste faintly acrid—smoky and earthy, like a good Islay scotch. It's not unpleasant, but it does have wariness tickling at the nape of my neck again. I still don't know why he's here.

"Why are you asking me about kissing and biting? Why were you watching me? More importantly, *why are you here?*"

"I was working up to that!" the ex-priest grumps, shifting on his feet again, and I realize that I've completely misread him from the start. He's not impatient at all.

He's *nervous.*

I slowly uncross my arms and watch as he takes a step forward, and then a step back, and then turns to face the ocean, and then turns back to me. And then finally he says, "I came to see if—maybe—if you're not busy or anything—and only if you'd like to—I mean, only if you *felt* like it—if you'd like to get dinner. With me. Sometime." The last words he grates out like they're physically painful to speak, and that proud face dips down to the floor as if he's considering curling up into a miserable ball after this display of vulnerability.

Everything I was feeling—the petulance, the suspicion, the amusement—everything is replaced by a drowsy, dulcet bloom of tenderness in my chest.

Well, okay, not everything. There's still a heady cocktail of sangria-fueled lust coursing through my veins, but it's not at odds with the tenderness at all. Instead the two feed each other, making my heart thump for this shy, nervous man as I throb elsewhere.

I take a step toward him, deciding that if he wants to get dinner, he's probably not going to be bothered by the state of my erection. "So you saw me kissing and biting someone last night, and instead of killing me like a good vampire hunter, you want to take me out on a date?" I say it lightly, but the words are blunt. I need to be sure.

He looks at me through eyelashes the color of angry rain. "I'm not a hunter anymore," he says simply.

"But you were watching me last night. That wasn't hunting?"

"I have a new job this week, private security on the island. Midnight patrol."

He is such a big guy that I'm not actually all that surprised. His size, plus the way he carries himself—like a man who's taken lives—would be enough of a deterrent for most touristy troublemakers, I'd imagine. Still though. "Priest to private security—not exactly adjacent vocations, my friend."

His shoulder moves the slightest bit—the world's

smallest shrug. "Finding work after the Church has been hard. The ... nighttime ... has stayed with me. The peering into shadows, the walking silently under the stars. It's a habit I can't break. So patrolling someplace in the dark seemed like a natural fit. I honestly wasn't looking for vampires. Just drunks or buggy thieves."

"But you found me anyway."

He blinks as if remembering. "I found you anyway. You were—you are—beautiful." He flushes again, looks away.

Beautiful. I've been called many flattering things before (because there's lots of flattering things about me, that's just facts) but it's been a long, long time since I've been called beautiful.

I study him as he looks out the window, the strong lines of his jaw and nose, the impossible color of his hair. The shy press of his full lips. I don't know this man's name, I don't know his secrets or his hopes or where he's from or where he sleeps at night or what he thinks about when he's alone. I only know that he's a bashful, grunting hulk of a man; I only know he used to kill my kind ... but for some reason, has chosen not to anymore.

I only know that he saw me kissing and biting someone last night, and instead of hunting me down out of a lingering sense of duty to humankind, he's here awkwardly asking me out on a date. Telling me he thinks I'm beautiful while I fuss at him over sangria.

The tenderness I'm feeling toward him is practically an undertow now. I'm being sucked into the deep.

"What's your name, former priest? And do you know

mine?"

His expression is careful when he looks at me. Guarded. "You go by Bastien."

Bastien is, in fact, my real name, and only someone who knows how to burrow into layers of paperwork would have found it on my lease here. "You were a hunter indeed," I murmur.

He nods, but he doesn't apologize, which I respect. And maybe even like? I have to admit, after centuries of prowling after people, it's rather nice to be prowled after myself.

"And I'm ..." The man hesitates, and I realize it's because he's unused to saying his first name. It makes me wonder how recently he's left the Church. "My name is Aaron."

I've wandered close enough to him that I could touch him now, if I wanted. I don't touch him, but I do enjoy the way his eyes rake down my taut stomach to where my pants hang low around my hips. He yanks his gaze back up as if embarrassed to be caught looking, but I don't miss how he angles his body ever so slightly away as if he doesn't want to frighten me with his body's response to mine.

I have never met a priest or hunter like him. A quiet brute who just wants dinner and maybe kissing. Maybe more ...

Maybe waking up this morning was a good idea after all.

"Okay, Aaron," I say softly. "I'll go to dinner with you."

CHAPTER 2

AARON

WHEN I WAS a young priest learning how to hunt vampires, our teachers warned us how beautiful vampires were, how beguiling, how they could bewitch the senses and thwart good sense just with a smile.

Well, here I am on a date with a vampire, utterly bewitched. Good sense thwarted past reckoning.

"More wine?" Bastien asks, tipping the bottle to my glass and topping it off before I can refuse. The fading sunlight limns him in red and pink and gold, and I'm trying not to stare, but it's impossible. His face is almost too lovely to be real—a Pre-Raphaelite composition of full lips and long eyelashes, large eyes and a Greek nose. His jaw is finely carved and his cheeks and forehead are aristocratically high, and he is all contrasts—sculpted features with soft, inviting lips, ivory-pale skin with dark eyes and hair.

He looks like a painting. Like he would have been in a painting when he was mortal.

"We're quite a sight, aren't we?" Bastien observes, setting the bottle down and picking up his own glass by the stem. His vowels curve with an accent I can't quite place—nearly French, nearly British, a fleeting glimpse into lifetimes he's spent on other shores. "A vampire and a priest, breaking bread."

Old habits have me glancing around, although we're in the far corner of the covered restaurant patio and well out of earshot of any other diners. When I look back to Bastien, his mouth is curled up at the edges.

"Worried the villagers will come knocking with torches and crosses later?" he asks, amused.

I make an affirmative grunt, and then I look down at my wineglass. "I didn't need any more wine."

"Yes, you did," Bastien says, the smile still toying at his lips. "How else will I get to know your deepest, darkest secrets?"

He's got a point. We've made it through the walk up to the restaurant and ordering our meal with me barely speaking at all. Because of one very embarrassing fact that I decide is best to confess to him now. "I don't have secrets. Or things to talk about. I'm not—I'm not interesting. Like you." I look down at the sunset-colored ocean below us as I say this, so I don't have to see the moment he decides this is a terrible, boring date and he's going to leave.

But he doesn't leave. And when he finally speaks, his richly musical voice is pitched very low and very soft, in a way that sends heat licking in my belly. "A former priest—a former vampire hunter—who saw a vampire being wicked and decided to get closer to wickedness instead of further away ... that sounds very interesting to me."

Closer to wickedness ... I almost shudder with the accuracy of his words. When I saw him kissing that man last night, when I saw the pleasure on the man's face as Bastien held him close and buried his mouth in the man's neck, I felt longing like I'd never felt it before. I felt the first real jolts of arousal since I'd left the priesthood.

I wanted it. I wanted kisses and biting. I wanted this vampire to do to me what I'd vowed I'd never let any vampire to do me, and drink my blood. In fact, I'd even worn a long-sleeved sweater—very, very thin, mind you, because even with the constant breeze, Hamilton Island is warm—because it has a low rounded collar that completely exposes my throat. I don't have the words or eloquence to tell Bastien what I want, but maybe he'll know it without me having to tell him. Maybe he'll take it without asking. Maybe he'll pin me in some dark corner somewhere and make me moan with pleasure the way he did to the man last night.

I dare to look back at Bastien. The smile is still there, but it's no longer a signal of amusement. It's a signal of something else ...

An invitation, maybe?

Or maybe I'm just seeing what I want to see. Maybe it's pity. Maybe I'm pitiable and pathetic, a clumsy, eager fool who wanted to get closer to something dangerous and beautiful and who's now made himself ridiculous.

I suddenly wish I'd worn a collared shirt. I look like a vampire's version of a tart.

Bastien sees I'm lost in my own mind, and he reaches for my hand. It takes me a minute to understand—it's been so long since I've been touched in kindness—and then even longer to accept. Bastien sees my hesitation but attributes it to something else. "We're safe here," he says softly. "I won't let anything happen to you."

His meaning is clear; this bright, touristy place does feel very safe, but safety is always conditional on whose hand you're holding, and where I grew up, this could still be dangerous. It's a particular kind of fear I didn't have to feel as a priest, but now it's here, as real as my desire for Bastien. I didn't realize I was afraid until he offered to help hold the fear with me.

I look down at our hands as he speaks, and then I have to look away. The sight of our fingers and palms—big and square and obviously male—touching is the most wonderful and the most terrifying thing I've ever seen. And his words ...

"Thank you," I manage to get out. The warmth and pressure of someone holding my hand, promising to keep me safe, is making my throat ache, and the words come out rough. "I'm not used to someone thinking they need to protect me. Because I'm so big," I add in order to explain, and Bastien laughs.

"I can see that. You are *very* big."

The words are flirtatious enough that I feel myself blushing. He laughs some more.

"You're very easy to tease, you know," he points out.

"I've made you blush like a virgin all day, and it's starting to make me wonder how long it's been since you've been on a date."

"I've never done this before," I admit in a mumble.

He grins, eyes sparkling. "A date with a vampire? I imagine not."

"No, Bastien. *This*." I look down at our hands and then to the wine and the table and the view.

A small line appears between his brows. "Aaron. Please tell me I'm not your first date."

I can't tell him that, so I don't say anything at all.

Bastien's grin fades, but his eyes remain intense. "Are you a virgin?"

I make a noise that could mean anything, but Bastien doesn't let me wriggle out of answering.

"I know it's an invasive question, but I'm a vampire, so humor me. How untouched is my laconic priest?"

The possessive *my* in *my laconic priest* makes my pulse thud a little harder, and Bastien's eyes rove over my exposed neck as I reply honestly. "Very, um, untouched," I admit.

He lifts his eyes back to mine and tugs his hand free. "Well then."

I stare down at my now-empty hand, feeling stupid, and I slowly pull it back into my lap. Maybe he doesn't like virgins. Maybe he doesn't like the reminder that I was a priest. Maybe—

"What do you say we skip dinner?" Bastien asks, interrupting my panicked self-recriminations. "I'll feed you at my house."

I blink at him. "What?"

He leans forward, a lock of hair tumbling over his forehead and his dark eyes flashing with some strong emotion I can't identify. "Aaron, I'm sitting across from a strapping ex-priest who's been flaunting his naked throat at me all evening, and now he tells me he's a virgin. The reins of my control are understandably snapping." He digs out some cash for the wine and tosses it on the table, and before I can say anything, he's taking my hand and hauling me easily to my feet and tugging me out the door.

Confused but also flattered and also hoping this means what I think it does, I follow Bastien, trying not to look like I'm getting dragged off to slake a vampire's obscene needs. My dick gives a heavy twitch at the thought, stirring and lengthening until I'm swollen enough that I have to adjust myself so I don't look like a walking teen-movie gag.

"When did you leave the priesthood?" Bastien asks once we're on the footpath back to his house. He's in a white button-down shirt, and the setting sun outlines all those flat, dense muscles underneath the fabric. He's built lithe and lean and graceful, and I have the sudden image of him crawling over me like a huge cat, eyes hot with hunger.

I'm too distracted to answer him. "I—what?"

Bastien sighs. "Look, I know learning you're virginal in the extreme should make me *more* careful with you, and probably we should have, like, five more dinner dates and some long talks about intimacy before I even think about touching you, but I'm a vampire, okay? I'm sorry, but I'm one of your sexy grunts away from taking your virginity in between some shrubs while the wallabies watch, and it's been a century or two since I've needed to fuck like this, and I'm barely hanging on, so what I need to happen right now is I need you to help distract me until we get back to my house and I can at least give you some privacy before I put my mouth all over you. Got it? Good. Now talk to me. When did you leave the priesthood?"

Too many feelings for me to process are crowding my chest and stomach. Lust and shyness and gratitude and fear and more fear.

So I just try not to think about all that and give him what he wants instead. It's easy, in a thrilling kind of way, to surrender to his bossiness. "I was officially dismissed from the clerical state four months ago. The Church was ... reluctant, I guess. There are not so many of us left now that they can easily let even one go."

"Not so many priests?" Bastien asks.

"Not so many priests who are trained as I was," I clarify.

"Ah, in the Order of Saint Marcellus, you mean," Bastien says, and I'm surprised.

"You're not supposed to know that name," I tell him.

Bastien makes a scoffing noise. "Vampires aren't supposed to know the name of the ancient order sworn to hunt them down?"

"It's supposed to be secret; we're forbidden to whisper it to anyone outside the order, even in the throes of death. Who did you learn it from?" I frown, thinking of all the reasons a priest of the Order might break his vow. "Did he tell you under duress?"

"You mean, did I torture it out of someone?" Bastien asks dryly. "No. I earned that knowledge honestly. How long were you a priest?"

"Ten years. What do you mean you earned it honestly?"

A wallaby hops across the road, stopping to look blankly at us and then moving along after a moment. Bastien watches it, his face growing distant. "It was a long time ago," he says finally, which doesn't really answer my question. "When I was mortal. Why did you become a priest?"

There it is again, that urge to do as he says. I answer him without worrying that I sound grunty or stupid or overeager, even though this is the most I've spoken aloud at one time in the last four months, and it feels strange. "I grew up in a small town an hour outside of Toowoomba. There're as many churches as there are houses, or so it felt like. Praying was in my blood, but so was fighting, and it felt like there was nowhere good a big, hot-blooded boy like me would end up, but my childhood priest wanted to help. He sent me to his mentor in Brisbane, and they promised if I went to seminary and was ordained, they'd find the right place for me. And that's how I ended up in Rome, inducted into the Order."

"Hmm," Bastien says. A warm breeze ruffles up the road, and when I look over, his shirt is clinging to every contour of his torso and chest. And his trousers are clinging too, and I see the distinct outline of a large erection—the same one I did my best not to gawk at this morning. Bastien wasn't lying about wanting me. And I want this vampire to want me. I want him to touch me and make me bleed and make me come. I want it so much my body hurts trying to hold all the wanting—and the terror of *who* I want—inside it.

"I think," Bastien says, "you've just explained the *how*. And not the why. Don't forget I can taste your belief, Aaron. You became a priest because you wanted to, not because it was the only choice you had, and I want to know why."

I grunt a little, not sure how to answer this. Somehow I know he won't settle for the short and easy answers I gave when I was in the process of ordination—the *I feel called* and *I want to serve God as much as I can*, the kinds of answers that are as expected as they are reductive. And I can't make a fool out of myself more than I already have.

I decide to give him the truth, as intimate and ephemeral as it is.

"I always knew I loved God," I explain, "because I always knew He loved me. When I was a boy, I would go out to my family's fields and watch the sky at night. We were way out in the bush, and there weren't any lights, and the sky was dripping with stars. So many stars that it felt like I could hold out my hand and they'd fall into my palm like rain. Like all I had to do was ask and God would fill my heart with stars like He filled the cisterns and wells and lakes with water, and who wouldn't want to serve a God like that?"

"Who indeed," Bastien murmurs, something tender

curling into his words. "Do you still believe that? That God will fill your heart with stars if you ask?"

"Yes."

"So the boy on the farm became a priest because he grew up with stars raining light on him night after night, and it felt like God Himself was covering him in a net of pure love." Bastien's voice is still tender, but it's tight too, as if he's upset. "There are many worse, and cheaper, reasons to become a priest, Aaron. My hat is off to you."

We turn onto the narrow road that leads to the expensive houses celebrities like to rent—a road I've patrolled a few times since starting my job here. Bastien doesn't say anything as we approach the discreet gates of his home, and I'm starting to feel like I've said something wrong.

"Bastien," I say, feeling clumsy with my words, as usual, "did I make you angry with me? By talking about God?"

Bastien lets out an indignant huff, and I almost smile. He's so *funny*, this bloodthirsty painting of a man, he's so open. It only took ten years of vampires and death to become a silent gargoyle, but that he's managed to live lifetimes and still be funny and honest and adorable—it's astonishing, really.

He punches in the code to his gate as he huffs some more, and then as he impatiently ushers me through, he says, "I'm not angry, Aaron."

"You're not?"

A self-deprecating puff of air. "I'm a little ashamed is all."

"Ashamed?"

"It's one thing to scent your earnestness," he says as we walk down the path to the door. Cockatoos ruffle and bitch as we walk by, but they sense in their animal way that Bastien is a predator, and so they give us a wide berth, fluttering from a distance. "But to hear it—to know it—Aaron, I don't think you appreciate how good you are. And if I weren't already going to hell on account of being an immortal cannibal, then I'd be going to hell for the mere fact that your goodness incites me to badness. It makes me want to do very depraved things with you. *To* you, actually, very much to you."

I don't think I can breathe. I want those depraved things so badly, but when I open my mouth to tell him so, all that comes out is a low noise of acknowledgment.

Luckily, Bastien doesn't seem to mind my taciturnity. He keeps going as he opens his front door. "I want to fuck your goodness. Do you understand how odd that is? I want to bite it. I want to drink these wonderful, earnest secrets of yours down as you shudder for me. I want to make you feel every dirty thing you've earned by being so good; I think you're too pure to be truly debased, but my God, I want to try."

The door swings open, and we step inside, and before I can react—which means it happens too fast for *any* human to react—I'm shoved against the wall and Bastien's mouth is on mine.

He pins me there with a forearm against my throat, his free hand roaming shamelessly around my body, sliding over my stomach and hips and then delving right past my waistband, sending my back arching far off the wall.

"Whoa, there," he says like I'm a stallion he's trying to break, and fuck if that doesn't get me hotter. All my life, my size has been something to be afraid of, something to be contained, but Bastien seems ... *delighted* by my bigness. *Pleased* by it. Aroused by it. Like it's thrilling for him to have a massive, wild male grunting and snarling at his touch. And for some reason, that makes it thrilling for me. He isn't scared of me, and he's just as strong, if not stronger. I don't have to worry about hurting him or scaring him, no matter how much I thrash or no matter how many snarls I make.

And I am snarling now as his clever fingers find my erection and squeeze before pushing lower to cup my testicles. His mouth on mine is firm and persuasive, coaxing me to open in between my growls, his kiss turning possessive as he strokes along my tongue and licks at the inside of my lips.

"What can't I do to you?" he whispers against me. His hand in my pants is wicked, and I've never felt anything like it, not even the times I've done this to myself. "Tell me, mon prêtre. What can't I do to you?"

I know he's honestly asking, and so I give him an honest answer. "Nothing."

"That's a dangerous thing to tell such a one as me."

"I watched you take care of a total stranger last night. You only took a little, and when you were done, he was conscious and smiling and safe. And you have every reason to hate me because of what I used to do, and yet you're still asking me permission now. I trust you, Bastien."

He goes still against me, and after a second, he pulls back enough that he can meet my stare, pulling his hand free from my pants too, which has me arching again. His eyes are so dark, so unreadable. His breath is warm against my kiss-damp mouth. "You truly trust me?"

"I do."

He closes his eyes. "Maybe you shouldn't."

"Are you going to kill me?"

"Jesus!" His eyes fly open. "Of course not, Aaron! What the *fuck*."

"Then I trust you," I say, shrugging against the wall. He lowers his forearm and takes a deep breath, running a hand down his face.

"Okay. Okay. I'm going to fuck you and I'm going to bite you and I'm going to play with your cock and maybe suck it too—not all in that order, obviously, I'm having a hard time thinking right now. It will feel good when I bite you and I won't take too much, but I need you to tell me if it's still too much or if it hurts. I mean, hurts in a bad way. You know what I mean."

Seeing this noble vampire all flushed and flustered—because of me—is gratifying beyond measure. "I trust you," I repeat simply. "As long as you don't mind that I—I don't know what I'm doing."

"Jesus Christ," Bastien mutters to himself, running another hand down his face. "Do I mind that this giant farm-boy-slash-priest is a virgin and trembles whenever I so much as hold his hand. *Jesus.*"

He presses back against me, one hand deftly unbuttoning my pants and freeing my erect organ. I hiss the moment it hits the cool air, and he hisses along with me as he looks down and sees I'm already wet at the tip.

"Am I the first person to touch this cock?" he asks me, his voice low and sounding more French than ever. "I think I must be. You're about to go off in my hand, and I haven't done anything yet. Fuck, that's sexy. Jesus, are you about to come right now? You really are. *Fuck* fuck fuck fuck—"

Bastien's husky wonder is the soundtrack to my first orgasm with someone else; all it takes is looking down and seeing him wrap those elegant fingers around my length and I am done for. He doesn't even squeeze me, he doesn't even stroke me—he *holds* me and I come immediately.

We both watch as thick ribbons of white spill from the tip and over his fingers, my erection visibly jerking with each and every surge. I'm ashamed, I'm so ashamed, but there's no stopping it, no stopping the heavy spurts desperate to leave my body. And even in the midst of my shame, it feels so *fucking good*, so good that I don't care how lewd I'm being, how I'm dirtying Bastien's hand and dripping onto his floor, I don't care, if someone tried to stop me before I was finished, I'd rip them in half, because I need to finish more than I need to take my next breath, that's how urgent and necessary this is.

Not that there's any possibility of stopping anyway. The surges are a mindless, animal pleasure, hooked deep into my belly, and by the time I'm spent in Bastien's hand, I barely know my own name. I couldn't have torn myself away from this moment even if I'd had bands of brother priests to help me, and it isn't until the uncivilized spilling stops that I realize I was grunting and pushing into Bastien's hand.

I go silent and still, feeling like a dirty beast.

Bastien looks up at me with something like shock, and I'm wondering if maybe he's never had a clumsy virgin come all over him before, and maybe he's disgusted by it—

Before I can even finish the thought, he's kissing me, devouring my mouth with skillful, pressing strokes, driving every other thought and worry from my mind. Between us, my exposed cock gives an eager kick, and he pulls back, lips swollen and pupils blown.

"I have to fuck you now," he says hoarsely.

"Okay," I agree, and then he grabs my hand and yanks me toward his bedroom. I manage to sort of tuck myself back together as we go, although the horse is rather out of the barn as far as pride goes at this point, given that I just came all over his floor after he did nothing more than hold me in his hand.

"That was the sexiest thing I've ever seen," he says, partially to himself as he tugs me along. "And I've seen a lot. My God, how am I going to do this. A *virgin*. Think, Bastien, think." He lets go of my hand to flap his own in a sort of vague, horny distress.

"Bastien," I say as we reach his bed.

"What?"

"I'm very big."

"I *know* that, Aaron, I just saw how big you are. Why do you think I'm in such a state?"

It's never occurred to me before that a vampire could be, well, cute, but there's something very cute about how fussy he is when it comes to his reactions to me. "No, I mean, I'm a strong bloke. Sturdy and tough, you know? And the Order—" I won't mention the grim endurance tests of pain and strength, because even in my limited experience, I know it wouldn't make good bedroom talk, so I settle for, "The Order made me even tougher. You can't hurt me." I think of the stranger Bastien drank from last night, his eyes fluttering in ecstasy as his hips mindlessly rolled against a vampire's. "I want you to be at your wickedest. *Please.*"

For a moment, Bastien looks almost young. Helpless with his own wanting. And then he's all vampire again, hungry and heavy-lidded. Very, very wicked as he unbuttons his shirt and lets it fall to the floor. The wickedest as he toes off his shoes and removes his socks and unbuttons his pants. The ruddy head of his erection peeps out above his zipper, swollen and dark against his pale stomach, and the fading sun over the ocean bathes his perfect form in pink and purple-hued light as he walks toward me.

"Clothes off," he says, not bothering with *please* or *thank you.* "Let me see this priest who needs to sin so badly."

With shaking hands, I do as he says, peeling off my sweater and shoes and pants. The bedroom has large glass doors that fold open, and the breeze comes right up off the water, sweet and soft and somewhere right between warm and cool. Shadows move through the room as the trees and shrubs outside rustle in the breeze, and by the time I'm naked, Bastien is in front of me, running appreciative hands all over my body like a shadow himself, like the actual darkness is beckoning me into an embrace.

And I go willingly.

"Down, sweet priest," he whispers, guiding me onto the bed, onto my back. "Down, down. Let me have a taste."

I expect his mouth on mine after that, or maybe even on my neck, but it's my stomach where I feel his kiss first, hungry and quick, and by the time I tense and gasp underneath it, he's already moved down to my navel, and then down the trail of hair to the base of my cock.

I'm not ready for it, not ready for how soft his mouth is, how wet, how it's almost like tickling but it's not, tickling isn't the right word at all.

"What can't I do to you," Bastien murmurs, almost to himself.

"Nothing," I whisper to the ceiling. And then his fangs sink into my erection.

It should hurt, and for the first instant it does, a spark of pain sizzling up my spine, but it's replaced immediately with pure, delicious pleasure as Bastien begins to suck. It's indecent, yes, so indecent, a vampire *there* doing *that*—it should be the ultimate boundary for a priest sworn to destroy vampires. But I'm not a priest anymore, and my body is aching down to the marrow for his sharp, bloody kiss. I don't know what kind of magic vampires possess—or if it's some biological mechanism designed to help them catch and keep prey—but his fangs feel *good*. An invasion, yes, but an invasion like his tongue in my mouth is an invasion, an invasion like his dark eyes in my mind are an invasion. And each suck—the *suck*—oh my God, it's almost better than coming itself, it's like Bastien is yanking pleasure out of my body, like he's drawing the very heart of me out through his bite.

And that it's on my cock...

"Fuuuck," Bastien says, wrenching himself away, his mouth bloody in the dark. I can feel the wet smear of where he was sucking me on my dick, and I'm harder than fucking ever. "*Fuck*. I could do that forever, do you understand? I could drink from your cock every night and never get sick of it. What are you doing to me? No, don't try to answer, I know you'll just grunt at me and then I won't have any more information than before you grunted. Don't move."

It's nearly dark outside, with only the last lavender blush of dusk and the pool lights outside to light the room, and so it's his silhouette I watch as he goes to a table by the bed and pulls out a small bottle.

"In case you don't already know, vampires can't carry human infections," Bastien says, coming back to the bed. "So we don't need protection."

"You're not worried about getting me pregnant?" I ask, and Bastien pauses between my legs, his head tilted.

"Aaron, did you just *make a joke*? You did! You made a joke! I'm so proud, I'm like your joke-father, except not really, that would be creepy, unless—I mean, if you want to call me *daddy*, I am not opposed to that at all, I think I could get used to Daddy Bastien if we worked on it."

I'm smiling at him, at the ebullience of him even with his dick jutting out from his hips and his mouth still wet with blood, and that's when I hear the bottle click open and then feel the slick press of his finger.

I grunt as my blood-smeared cock gives a leap. A hot feeling knots itself tight in my belly, low down, and it cinches my balls up to my body.

"My virgin priest," Bastien croons, adding another finger. He does something—presses somewhere—and a groan tears out of my chest. My hips leave the bed as I follow some unknown instinct and try to fuck up in the air, needing more, needing to fuck or be fucked or anything really, so long as it's *more*.

"I'm giving you my cock now, mon prêtre. Open for me—yes, like that—do you feel me against you? That's it, yes, breathe, breathe, my wonderful seeker of wickedness. Oh, I love how you squirm, I love how those powerful hips buck for me. Yes, almost there, breathe, breathe. Do you feel me, sweetheart? I feel you, and you feel like a hot fist clenched around my shaft. I'm not going to last long, not with you, you sweet, brutal man. Fuck."

It's like being split in two but in the best possible way. Bastien is so much bigger than his fingers, and the power behind each and every stroke is enough to make me grunt even though he's going slow. He moves between my thighs with sleek, near-cruel strength, but I love it. I'm throbbing into the cool ocean air with how good it feels to be underneath this vampire, and each stroke is hitting me someplace deep inside that has my grunts getting louder, longer, lower.

"It's happening again," I moan. "It's gonna— I'm gonna—"

He lunges forward, fangs shining in the shadows, and right as I begin the shameful spurting again, his face is in my neck and he's biting me and drinking me down. The sheer, intoxicating pleasure of his bite coupled with the possessive invasion of him inside me—I feel ridden, I feel owned, I feel dirty and wild and seen. I feel like I want this forever, this exact moment, Bastien buried inside me, both fang and cock, while my own cock throbs and spills between our stomachs.

And it's as he's drinking me that his own orgasm begins jolting inside my arse, as if the pleasure of tasting me has pushed him over the edge, and he sucks his fill as his hips keep fucking and fucking and fucking, shoving into me with a desperation that drives my own climax further and further on, spattering again and again between us both.

Minutes go by, and then hours. Eternities. Both of us caught in a dizzying world of bleeding, primal orgasms. Until finally Bastien lifts his head and hisses his deep, predatory satisfaction into the dark.

The sound warms up the inside of my chest. I satisfied him. I've felt more alive tonight than I have in years, I've found the wicked ecstasy I came here looking for— and yet the thing that has me smiling at the ceiling is that I've pleased him.

He notices. "You like being my toy?" he murmurs, nuzzling into my bloody neck and kissing it, licking it clean. "My personal priest toy? Hmm?"

"Yes," I grunt. I turn so he has to look at me. "I—I want to do it again."

He laughs a little, kissing my lips and then draping himself on top of me. "We need to wait a while before I drink from you again. Maybe a day or two. But everything else ..."

Hope is scarier than being bitten by a vampire, but I let myself feel it. "You want to see me in a day or two?"

Bastien's ribs heave against mine, and I can't tell if he's laughing at me or if it's one of those self-deprecating laughs for himself. "Aaron," he says, "I don't want to frighten you, but I'm already trying to figure out how I can marry you, or at least keep you locked up naked for my pleasure for the next decade. Yes, I want to see you in a day or two. And a month or two. And a year or two. I have nowhere else to be, and you're the best thing I've found in more than two hundred years. So by all means, consider yourself penciled in."

"Oh," I say. It's about all I can say. I'm feeling too many things to say anything more. Except. "I was a priest in the Order, Bastien. I want this more than you can know, but ... our pasts ..."

Bastien kisses my chest, his hips beginning a gentle war of pressure and friction as he does. "I'll tell you a secret, mon prêtre," he murmurs. "I was a priest too."

For a moment, there is only the sound of the ocean

outside. I can't think. I can't even breathe, I'm so stunned. "You were a priest?" I manage.

"I joined during la revolution," he says between presses of his lips to my skin. "Because I was terrified. I was the pointless, wastrel son of a comte, and I felt certain I'd be thrown in prison or worse, so I left the Second Estate for the First for no better reason than I was scared of my own bloodline and what it meant. I was asked to join the Order not long after, which I did, and was sent back to Paris to hunt vampires. There were many there that decade, drawn by the slaughter, and there were many vicious, murdering ones that I still don't regret killing. But all it took was one faster than me, one cleverer, and then I was at her mercy, and she drank from me, of course, that unforgivable sin for the Order. She gave me a choice, after—she could let me go back to the Church, where I would have to lie for the rest of my life about being bitten, or she could turn me. I only knew panic then; I was still chasing after some idea of safety. I didn't know I would be trading a short, lonely life for a long, lonely one, or I might have chosen differently, you see."

Bastien falls into silence then, and my chest hurts for him. I wrap my arms around him and brace my heels, and flip us over, so I'm caging him in.

"Christ, you're big," he mutters, but it's with delight as he runs both his hands over my bum and hips and back. My cock likes it when I'm patted and stroked like a prized stud, I guess, because it's all the way hard again, aching a little but ready for more. I rub it against his fresh erection, and we both groan.

"Bastien, I don't want you to be lonely," I say.

"It was maudlin of me to phrase it that way. I'm not lonely right now."

"No." I try again, searching for better words. "I'm not going to let you be lonely. Starting now. I want—I want to be tied to your bed. Married to you. I want your teeth in my neck whenever you're thirsty. I want it, and you've said that I've earned every dirty thing I want by being so good, so I've earned this and I'm taking it."

Bastien's eyes glitter in the dark. "So you are, mon prêtre. So you shall." He sounds happy and hopeful and just as scared as me, and yes, it's undeniable now, I'm falling in love with a vampire. "And if you are to be mine for all these months and years, what shall I do with you next?" he asks.

I rub my cock along the length of his, making us both shiver. "I think I have a few ideas," I tease.

"Look at you," Bastien says proudly. "One day with me and you're making jokes and smiling! You're the blithe one, my friend, yes, you are."

I lean down to kiss his beautiful mouth, and I can still taste blood between us. "I think you mean *sanguine*," I say, and then as we're still laughing, Bastien reaches for the bottle and the night sharpens once again into wonderful, wicked desire.

And it doesn't escape my notice that as Bastien worships me into sweet oblivion, the stars outside are raining down light over the sea.

The end.

Want more queer paranormal romance from Sierra Simone?

Keep reading for a taste of The Fae Queen's Captive!

A SNEAK PEEK AT THE FAE QUEEN'S CAPTIVE!

THE FAE QUEEN'S CAPTIVE

The Stag Court hall is lofty, although its recesses doesn't disappear into darkness like so many ceilings do here. Instead, I can see it high above us, ribbed with hammer beams, rafters, braces. Each hammer beam is carved with the figure of a running stag so that it looks as if the entire roof of the castle rests on their cobwebbed backs. Just as in the library, threads of mycelium twist around the rafters and the chains of the chandeliers, glowing a pale silver in the gloom.

The walls are made of dark wood but are covered in living heather and gorse, the gorse blown butter yellow with red and orange leaves caught among its thorns. Moss clings to corners, and a low fog swirls just above the flagged floor, which is mostly covered in rush mats and strewn with fresh herbs.

The hall is filled with revelers feasting, toasting, and dancing, and I see immediately that they are not mortal, that they are impossible, that they are figures from children's stories and art prints purchased at renaissance festivals. They are at turns horned, winged, hoofed—some have hair the color of jewels and flowers—some have extra joints, others have too-long limbs—some have eyes that are too large and teeth that are too sharp. Some look *almost* mortal, like Morven and Maynard and Idalia, but they are so beautiful that a feeling of inhumanity lingers about them nonetheless.

And at any rate, this is no human banquet, at least not one I've ever seen or studied the likes of, because there is a real, honest-to-god *orgy* happening in front of the queen.

My pulse kicks up as we approach, and I get a good look at the array before us. Seven or eight fairies are knotted into a skein of spread limbs and arched necks, and the music of their fucking rivals the eerie music of the musicians. One fairy's wings shiver in pleasure as she sits atop another fairy's face. Something shimmering falls from her wings as she does, dusting her partner and the people fucking behind her too.

I shiver along with those wings. I want to be her, with her, under her. I want to see if an insatiable girl could get enough on that platform with them all.

The queen for her part seems unmoved by the display of hedonism in front of her or by any of the ancillary displays happening at the long tables and in the fog-bathed corners of the room. Her posture is gracefully erect, and her hands rest without either stiffness or restlessness on the arms of her throne, but she's as still as the rest of the room is not, and her gaze is remote and cool, as if her mind is on other things. I don't see how it could be—I've only been in this hall for ten seconds, and already I want to plonk down and watch everyone cavort and play for the next hundred years—but perhaps she's used to it. Or perhaps she expects it. It is her court to hold after all.

Bright but haunting music plays from a corner—played by instruments I've seen more often in manuscripts than I have in real life: lutes and crumhorns and tabors.

I never imagined I would see them in real life next to a flipping *fairy orgy*, but there you are.

"Tonight begins the feast of Samhain," Felipe says in a low voice as he escorts me deeper into the hall. We pass a table with a horned fairy bent over its surface, his partner's hand on the back of his head to hold him down. His horns scratch the glossy wood as he's rutted into from behind, but when he catches me looking at him with concern, he gives me a feral smile. My heart kicks up another beat.

"Magic is stronger at Samhain," Felipe continues as we keep walking toward the throne. "And so are they. More dangerous too. More"—he seems to search for the right word—"*avid*. Take care."

Avid.

I glance around at the drinking and eating and dancing and fucking. Especially the fucking. It's as present as the smell of delicious food, as persistent as the music filling the hall.

I don't think I'll mind *avid* so much. It seems a lot like *insatiable*, and hell, if I have to be an abductee in fairyland, maybe I'll at least get to indulge myself a little. Or a lot.

My eyes slide back to the platform and then to the horned fairy being taken from behind.

Yes, *a lot* sounds very good at the moment.

"And I forgot to mention," Felipe says, and his voice is quicker now, more urgent, "that the fairy fruit that's written of in our world—"

"Yes, yes, I know," I say. "Don't eat the fruit."

Although when I glance around the hall again, it's hard to see what fruit the stories are talking about. There are piles of apples, bright red and shiny, and heaps of sloe berries, blackberries, raspberries, and plums. There are currants and hazelnuts and roasted chestnuts, and wines and meads in clear pitchers, all in familiar shades of red and pink and pale gold. It all looks delicious, fruits and fruit drinks perfect for a harvest festival, but none of it looks remotely magical. Definitely not like the fairy-MDMA the stories make fairy fruit out to be.

"If only it were that simple," Felipe says, his voice getting even lower as we skirt the platform currently occupied with a fairy sex fest. But he sounds no less urgent. "The fairy fruit is not..."

But he stops, and when I glance over at him, I find the ancient Spaniard is *blushing*.

"Salt," he manages after a moment. "Mortal salt will fix almost anything."

I sense that he wants to say more but can't or won't find the words, and it doesn't matter now, because we're almost to the edge of the sex platform and to the dais where the queen sits.

Her throne is made of the same dark wood as the walls of the hall and is carved into the likeness of two stags standing amidst waving ferns, their proud wooden heads studded with real antlers, which twist and stretch into a web of bone above the queen's head. The queen's crown too is made of antlers, although they are far slenderer than the ones mounted on the throne. They twist once above her brow, and there are only a few thin branches spraying off from the main circle of the crown. I notice the tines are sharp enough to promise blood.

"Your Majesty," Felipe says as we finally clear the orgy and come to the foot of the throne. Letting go of my hand, he sinks to one knee with his hand over his heart, just as Maynard and the others did earlier in the library. A second too late, I follow, not nearly as practiced, but the long gown I'm wearing hiding the worst of it, I think.

"I hope you are having a good Samhain," the Spaniard continues. Out of the corner of my eye, I see his gaze is cast politely to the ground. "I found your guest and have brought her to you."

"My many thanks," the queen says in Latin. "And you may rise."

I'm not sure if I'm supposed to keep my eyes on the ground even after coming to my feet, but American that I am, my instinct is to make eye contact. Although when I do, I wish I were kneeling again.

The queen's eyes, although still cool as ever, are like the dark water under a new moon, promising eternity, promising endless, endless forever. And when they meet mine, I suddenly feel like that eternity already knows me, already sees me—sees too much of me.

I think it's fear that doses my blood then, but there are so many things like fear that speed the heart, and I don't want her to see that I'm breathing faster, shallower. Not if I'm supposed to take care, stay clever. To hide, I drop my gaze to her dramatic mouth and then to the rest of her. She's wearing a different dress now, a long-sleeved gown made of a black silk the same endless color as her eyes, its bodice dropping in a sharp V to just above her navel. I can see the contour of her clavicle, the inner curves of her breasts before they disappear behind the raw silk edge of the bodice. I can see the faint undulation of her breastbone, only visible as a suggestion in the fickle light of the chandeliers.

Aside from a gold signet ring on her smallest finger, she is otherwise free of jewels and gems, which seems strange for a queen, but I also can't imagine a necklace more finely wrought than the delicate berm of her collarbone, a pendant more exquisitely shaped than the stretch of her exposed sternum.

"Janneth," the queen says. "Sit next to me, please. Felipe, you may leave us."

I look over at Felipe, who gives me a look that suddenly reminds me very much of how Dr. Siska looks at students who plan on closing down a pub for a night. Like he's trying to beam the words *please be careful* right into my mind.

I can't imagine he ended up trapped here at the Stag Court for four hundred years because he was careful.

Still, I'm a little—okay, a lot—unnerved when he bows and takes his leave and I'm up on the dais alone with the queen. She indicates the undecorated chair next to her, which is made of the same wood as hers but carved only with the antler motifs, not in the likeness of the stags themselves. I sit, my heart pounding, trying to remember everything Felipe told me.

Fairies can't lie. Mortals need to eat salt. Bargain for my safety for the duration of my stay...I suppose with the queen, but as I steal a glance over at her, I have no idea what I could possibly offer her that she doesn't already have. She's a queen of a magic and seemingly immortal realm, with an entire court of orgy enthusiasts. Unless she needs a horny archaeologist at her disposal, I'm useless.

"So, Janneth Carter," the queen says in English, not looking at me. Her gaze is on the court, and from this angle, I can see the minute flicker of her stare. Far from being uninterested, she's absorbing everything, marking every laugh and moan. "I see you have met Felipe. I presume you no longer believe this to be a dream?"

"It seems safer to act as if everything is real and that everything matters. But I still find it all hard to believe," I answer honestly.

The queen keeps her eyes on the courtiers in front of us, but I see the small lift of her eyebrow. "You, who sift through mud and rocks hoping to find treasure, find this hard to believe? I should think you would be constructed entirely of belief, given your vocation."

I used to be, and I almost tell her that. I almost tell her that there used to be a Janneth who believed in everything. But I can't find the words.

It's bad enough to be insatiable, but to have been naive too? Gullible? I wouldn't want to admit that eagerness to anyone, much less a person as coldly regal as the queen.

"What do you want with me?" I ask instead. It might not be polite to do so, and it's certainly not strategic, but if I'm going to make it back home after my kidnapping sentence is over, I should probably get a sense of why I was taken in the first place.

My abruptness doesn't seem to bother the queen. Her tone of voice is the same as it was before when she says, "What do you think we want with you?"

"Morven said—" Even though I'm looking at countless people fucking in front of me right now, the words are still strange to say. "I'm to be a toy. That mortal toys are more fun."

The strange feeling is shame, I realize, but not humiliation at the prospect of being a toy. No, it's shame at how much the idea quickens heat inside me. Even the word *toy* has my thighs pressing together under the star-stitched skirt of my gown.

"Morven said that, did he?" the queen says, not seeming to expect an answer. "Interesting."

"It isn't true, then?" I ask. I can't tell if I sound hopeful or disappointed.

"Nothing is true until it is," the queen responds. The fairies really don't like giving straight answers. "But there is a tradition in Faerie, of mortals being taken at times when the veil is thin. Many are taken to be consorts to a lord or lady of Faerie. For a time."

"Is that why I was taken?"

The queen turns to look at me, her long, thick hair sliding over her shoulder as she does. She doesn't speak, but her eyes burn their way up my body, seeking out the corset-plumped curves of my breasts and the exposed flesh of my throat.

They stay the longest on my lips, and the longer she stares at my mouth, the hotter and hotter I feel, like a fever is burning inside me.

"Your Majesty," someone says from the floor below the dais, tearing us away from the moment. The queen and I both turn to look, and even though I shouldn't be surprised by anything anymore, I am shocked at the sight of him. He is impossibly slender, with pink-purple hair and green skin. He wears a collar of spiked leaves over a gold velvet jacket and hose.

When he sees he has our attention, he gives a bow.

"You flatter this servant to grace him with your attention. I come bearing a gift from the Queen of the Thistle Court, and I would have your permission to give it to you as a symbol of her friendship."

"Is that so?" the queen asks. Her hair shimmers as she leans forward on the throne. "Let's see it, then."

With a smile sharper than the leaves of his collar, the man from the Thistle Court pulls a small, silk-covered bundle from his pocket. He unwraps the bundle to reveal a delicate bracelet made of silver-set gems. They wink pink and purple and green in the light of the hall.

"My lady gives this to you as a token of her feelings," the servant says, stepping forward and giving another bow. He holds out both hands, the bracelet cradled in the silk it came in. "It is yours."

"The Court of Stags and the Court of Thistles used to be united, did they not?" the queen says. She doesn't move to take the bracelet, but she's still leaning forward, as if very interested in the servant and his gift.

"Yes, Your Majesty. A very long time ago, I believe."

"More than centuries," says the queen. "More than ages, if the stories are to be believed. My great-grandmother had not yet been born, and the mortals outside our veil had not yet had their Christ."

The servant, while perhaps not expecting this digression, pivots smoothly. "And yet the Thistle Court will always and with great feeling remember the time our courts were as one."

"Oh," says the queen mildly, "I believe it. Put on the bracelet, please. I should like to see my gift on display."

For the first time, I see uncertainty hiccup through the servant. "Your Majesty, it would not be becoming for a lowly one such as myself to think of wearing such a—"

"Put on the bracelet," says the queen again, her voice still mild. But from nowhere, I see several fairies in russet-and-gold livery step forward. They have swords at their hips and pikes in their hands. The pikes are currently pointed straight at the ceiling, but the message is clear. The queen is not making a request.

The man from the Thistle Court swallows a final time. "Your Majesty," he whispers, but he seems to know his protests will get him nowhere but poked full of pike holes.

For my part, I'm not sure why he's so hesitant. Maybe it's some baroque court etiquette thing to not wear someone else's gift? But it's a simple enough choice: put on some jewelry, or get run through by a bunch of guards with very mean faces. Not that I understand why the queen is threatening him with pikes at all.

I shift uneasily on my seat, remembering once again Felipe's warnings about bargaining for safety.

With a shaking hand, the servant lifts the bracelet out of the silk and drapes it over his wrist. He's trembling so hard that the bracelet shivers over his skin, and then when he finally clasps the bracelet shut, he stumbles to the ground. At first I think it's because he's lost his balance or that he's perhaps thrown himself to the ground as a plea for mercy, but then a low tearing noise claws its way out of his throat, and I see he's gone taut with some kind of wordless agony.

The noise turns into a scream as thorns slowly push through his flesh, not big curved ones that grow on the stems of roses but thin ones growing as close together as barbs on a feather. Green liquid runs in narrow rivulets down his face, stains the white shirt pulled through the slashed silk of his jacket sleeves, drips off the long leaves of his collar.

It's his blood, I realize, far too late. He's bleeding all over from thousands of these thorn wounds, and it's because of—

The bracelet. The bracelet somehow did this.

I stand to—well, I don't know what I'm going to do—but a guard steps in front of me and gives me a forbidding look. I am not allowed to help. To interfere.

Shocked, I turn to stare at the queen. For her part, she seems completely unmoved, her expression unchanged by the man writhing in unimaginable pain before her feet. She watches him scream and bleed with almost nothing on her face, nothing at all, and there's no compassion at all in the slow, deliberate way she raises her hand.

One of her court guards goes to the servant and removes the bracelet from the servant. The thorns retreat, leaving so, so much viridian blood behind. It pools beneath him.

"Take the bracelet away from here," says the queen, voice as even as ever. "And take *him* to the dungeons."

The guards obey, expressions neutral as they heave the now-whimpering man from the floor and grab him by the wrists and ankles. The bracelet is carefully collected and carried behind the man it nearly killed. His blood is left there, shining slick and green.

The court—which had paused to watch the show—now returns to feasting with gusto, the music striking up even louder, the dancers laughing, the lovers moaning. It's not as if it hasn't happened. It's as if it happening energized them. It's as if it happening was exciting and good.

And that's when the fear comes back, a wave of it so heavy that I think I might drown. I sit, stunned and sick.

"You knew something was wrong with it," I say numbly to the queen, who's now settled back on the throne. A small smile haunts her lips—the first smile I've seen from her.

It's beautiful. And terrifying.

"Of course, I knew," replies the queen, looking out at her reveling court, reveling all the harder with blood spilled on the floor. Some even come forward and drag their fingertips through it before sucking their hands clean with relish or offering their fingers to lovers to lick clean. Green smears their mouths and drips down their chins.

The fear is a thousand tiny bugs crawling on the inside of my skin now.

"But how? He said—" I think back to the servant's words, trying to filter through exactly what he said and how he phrased it. "He spoke of friendship. And Felipe told me fairies can't lie."

"The *friendship* between my court and the Court of Thistles is one marked by cairns and crow-circled battlefields. A token of their lady's feelings would only be something meant to make me suffer. You look surprised, Janneth, but I suppose it's good that you see this now: there are more ways to lie than just with words."

I can't believe she's talking to me so calmly, so levelly, after watching that fairy screaming and punctured on the floor. I can't believe I'm talking back to her.

And that's not the worst of it, actually. The worst is

that I'm not sure how I feel about watching that fairy bleed, because if the queen had not asked him to put on that bracelet—if she had not seen through the trick—then it would have been her bleeding. Her screaming.

And I do not like that thought either.

I like it even less.

"I'm sorry," I say, still numb. "I'm sorry they tried to hurt you."

"Do not be," says the queen dismissively. "I'm yet unafraid of the Thistle Court and its lady. Although I am insulted that she thought I wouldn't see through that little trick of hers. But perhaps returning the bracelet to her with her servant's severed hand inside it will remind her to try harder to kill me."

The remark about the servant's severed hand is so casually, effortlessly *cruel* that I have a moment where I don't fully understand it, where I think I must have misheard.

But I know I didn't.

And I know I'm not imagining that the queen is in a slightly better mood now. Her mouth is softer, as if her smile might return, and I see her long fingers move in time with the music. She's happy. There's blood on the floor and on the mouths of her people, and she's happy.

I take a deep breath and look down at my own hands. They are attached to my body, and they aren't covered in thorns or blood. For now. It's becoming very clear to me that I don't have any way to predict the caprice and cruelty of this place. Of the fairies here. Of *her*. It could be me screaming on the floor next, and as I look around the room at the banquet, I feel the creeping sense that any one of these people could be the ones to do it, to make me scream. Even if they didn't hurt me, they would watch. They would do nothing to help.

You should not feel safe. Message received, Felipe. Loud and clear.

The folk here love a bargain above all else; they love price.

You might be able to buy some safety that way.

I see the necessity of it even more now. If a bargain is what it takes to keep me safe until I figure out how to escape or Samhain ends and I'm sent back home, then a bargain is what I shall strike.

Although, fuck me, what can I offer? Sex? I'm not averse in the least to bargaining with sex—I like to have it, and being in the queen's bed sounds *amazing*. But the orgy platform in front of me is full of fairies flexible enough to put circus performers to shame, and sex is free for the taking everywhere else in the room. I can't see how sex with me would be a very tempting offer. Like offering a nickel to a billionaire.

Think, Janneth. Think.

I could talk to her about excavation strategies, I guess. Demonstrate how to make tea on a dig site with nothing but a camping stove and a willingness to get burned. What a fairy queen would want with that information, I don't know, but it's all I've got. I don't know how to fight or enchant bracelets; I don't know how to do anything other than like history and sex and crave more from life than life can possibly give me. I'm just a mortal girl in fairyland, with nothing but myself to offer.

But maybe that's it? Morven had said mortal toys were more fun, after all, and the way the queen had looked at me when we were talking of consorts…

Well, I will never know if I don't try, and if I don't try, I might end up bleeding on the floor. So.

"Your Majesty," I say, knowing I sound a little clumsy saying the courtly words but forging ahead anyway, "I want to make a bargain with you."

This catches her attention, because for the first time at the banquet, she truly looks at me. "A bargain, Janneth Carter?"

Her voice is soft, dangerous even, but I continue, "Surely better than a stolen mortal consort is a mortal happy to be one. Guarantee me that you will add my safety to the promise you made in the library, and in return, I'll promise my willingness to you. To be your companion, your consort. To be whatever you wish until Samhain is over."

"Even if what I wish for is not a companion or consort?" Her voice is silky. "Even if I wish for a toy or a pet instead?"

I have the sudden image of being curled naked at her feet, her long fingers stroking my hair. I swallow.

"Then I will be your pet."

"And remind me of this promise I made in the library?"

"That I will stay here for two nights, and then on the

third, you'll let me leave Faerie. All I'm asking for is that you promise my safety too."

The queen gives me an appraising look, as if sifting through my words. Then she turns and gestures at her court, at the sex and excess, at the glinting jewels and sweat-shimmered skin. "And what, Janneth Carter, can you give me that I do not already have at a wave of my hand? You say you will offer me your willingness, but that is not in short supply here. Do you think the people at my court would be unwilling to come to my bed?"

"No, Your Majesty."

"So again, I ask: What can you truly offer me for this additional promise?"

I know that it's important that I do not lie, so I can't make up an answer for her. I can't invent something out of thin air. It needs to be the truth, but now I'm right back where I started, because the truth is that I have nothing at all to offer a queen like this one—

My eyes land on the orgy in front of me, on the twisting, moving bodies. But now I'm looking past the moving hands and hips, past the spread thighs and braced knees. I see the fairies' faces: their glazed eyes, their bored expressions. And with that in mind, the slow caresses and even slower kisses take on a new meaning. Not *savoring* slow but *desultory* slow. Not lingering but uninterested.

Maybe an immortal lifetime filled with every kind of pleasure does that to someone; maybe it's possibly to eventually become blasé about what some people crave beyond all reason.

But I think I'm personally a very, very long way from

that *maybe*. So long that it might take an eternity for me to be sated.

"I will always want more," I say, turning back to look at her. "That's what I can offer. I will always, *always* want more."

Her attention is wholly on me now. "Oh?"

She doesn't believe me, I think. There's a slight arch to her brow, a skeptical tilt of her head. I imagine she's seen enough people grow bored with indulgence to think I'm spinning tales, childishly asserting things I cannot possibly know about what *always* will mean to me.

And in one way, she might be right to doubt, because I can't know what *always* will mean to me. But I do know *me*—I know who Janneth Carter, horny archaeologist, is.

And if there was ever a time for insatiability to be a superpower, then this is it.

I stand and meet the queen's stare, pretending I know exactly what the fuck I'm doing.

"I'll prove it," I say lightly and step off the dais.

WANT MORE SHORT AND SPICY TREATS?

Like all things dark and paranormal?

Check out *The Fae Queen's Captive*, a dark sapphic standalone about an archeologist who's kidnapped by a ruthless fairy queen...

Save some of your screams for the queen, there's a good girl...

Janneth Carter has given up on magic these days. She's done being curious, insatiable, dreamy; she just wants to finish her graduate degree and spend the rest of her life as a sensible archeologist. So the last thing she expects when she goes to her dig site on Halloween night is three mysterious strangers standing outside an ancient Scottish grave.

Okay, well the *actual* last thing she expects is for those strangers to kidnap her and drag her into fairyland.

Once in the vivid, carnal world of Faerie, Janneth is at the mercy of the coldly lovely and incredibly cruel Stag Queen. Desperate to get home to her own world, she offers the Queen a bargain: she'll be a willing captive, the queen's pet, so long as the Queen promises to keep her safe until Janneth leaves Faerie.

But fae promises are complicated things, and nothing in Faerie, even pleasure—even love—comes without a price...

***The Fae Queen's Captive* is available everywhere as an ebook and in print!**

Craving more grumpy/sunshine gay romance?

Check out *Snow Place Like LA,* a second-chance romance about a costume designer who works on both porn costumes *and* costumes for wholesome Christmas movies and the sexy, glasses-wearing artist who broke his heart...

Cowritten by #1 *New York Times* bestselling

WANT MORE SHORT AND SPICY TREATS?

author Julie Murphy and *USA Today* best-selling author Sierra Simone—a steamy second chance Christmas in July rom-com.

After Angel and Luca connected on the set of *Duke the Halls* and had a whirlwind romance in the literal snow globe of Christmas Notch, Vermont, Luca found himself falling in love. Hard. He'd never been one to believe in fate or true love, but one thing was certain: Angel was his person. He knew it as well as he knew the history of American figure skating.

But when Angel left for an art school semester abroad without a word, Luca's already brittle heart was broken. No one ghosted Luca. Unless he was in a haunted house.

But with the spring semester long over, Angel is back home in Los Angeles for the summer, and unfortunately for Luca, this big town is turning out to be smaller than either of them ever expected...

***Snow Place Like LA* is available everywhere in ebook, print, and audiobook!**

ALSO BY SIERRA SIMONE

Co-Written with Julie Murphy:

A Merry Little Meet Cute

Snow Place Like LA: A Christmas in July Novella

A Holly Jolly Ever After

Seas and Greetings

A Jingle Bell Mingle

The Lyonesse Trilogy:

Salt in the Wound (a free Lyonesse prequel!)

Salt Kiss

Honey Cut

Bitter Burn

Standalones:

Red & White: an FFM winter story — FREE!

Supplicant: an age gap novella

Sanguine: an MM vampire story

Sherwood: an FFM novella

My Present This Year: a forbidden Christmas story - FREE!

The Fae Queen's Captive: a dark sapphic romance

The Priest Series:

Priest

Midnight Mass: A Priest Novella

Sinner

Saint

Thornchapel:

A Lesson in Thorns

Feast of Sparks

Harvest of Sighs

Door of Bruises

Misadventures:

Misadventures with a Professor

Misadventures of a Curvy Girl

Misadventures in Blue

The New Camelot Trilogy:

American Queen

American Prince

American King

The Moon (Merlin's Novella)

American Squire (A Thornchapel and New Camelot Crossover)

High Spice Historicals:

The Markham Hall Series

The Awakening of Ivy Leavold
The Education of Ivy Leavold
The Punishment of Ivy Leavold

The London Lovers
The Seduction of Molly O'Flaherty
The Wedding of Molly O'Flaherty

Far Hope Stories
The Chasing of Eleanor Vane
The Last Crimes of Peregrine Hind
The Conquering of Tate the Pious

Co-Written with Laurelin Paige

Porn Star

Hot Cop

ABOUT THE AUTHOR

Sierra Simone is a USA Today bestselling former librarian who spent too much time reading romance novels at the information desk. She lives with her husband and family in Kansas City.

Sign up for her newsletter to be notified of releases, books going on sale, events, and other news!

www.thesierrasimone.com
thesierrasimone@gmail.com